Growing Pains

For Peter, Kate, and for Connor, whose empathy and kindness inspired this story.
— A.M.

For the Queen of all Nannas, Audrey Ritchens. Thank-you for being the strongest and most inspiring human; I am so grateful to be your Granddaughter. XO
— M.J.

First published 2021

EK Books
an imprint of Exisle Publishing Pty Ltd
PO Box 864, Chatswood, NSW 2057, Australia
226 High Street, Dunedin, 9016, New Zealand
www.ekbooks.org

Copyright © 2021 in text: Alison McLennan
Copyright © 2021 in illustrations: Melissa Johns

Alison McLennan and Melissa Johns assert the moral right to be identified as the creators of this work.

All rights reserved. Except for short extracts for the purpose of review, no part of this book may be reproduced, stored in a retrieval system or transmitted in any form or by any means, whether electronic, mechanical, photocopying, recording or otherwise, without prior written permission from the publisher.

A CiP record for this book is available from the National Library of Australia.

ISBN 978-1-925820-52-2

Designed by Mark Thacker
Typeset in Minya Nouvelle regular 17 on 25pt
Printed in China

This book uses paper sourced under ISO 14001 guidelines from well-managed forests and other controlled sources.

10 9 8 7 6 5 4 3 2 1

Growing Pains

Alison McLennan & Melissa Johns

Do trees get cold, Finn wondered?

Earlier that morning, he'd shivered as he ran around in circles, pretending to be a fire-breathing dragon.

His mother made him come inside when real smoke came out of his mouth.
Rrraaahh!!
Now, as Finn sat staring out the window, trapped like a bear in a cage, he wondered if trees felt the cold.

They had planted the tree yesterday and now Finn was worried. What if it was freezing but couldn't tell anyone because it couldn't talk?

He rummaged through his drawers until he found the woolly scarf he was looking for. This would keep his tree warm.

When his mother was busy in the kitchen, Finn snuck outside and wrapped his arms around the tree.

'I'm sorry,' whispered Finn. 'I didn't know.'

He wound the scarf around the trunk and carefully tied it in a knot.

'You can keep it if you like,' he said. 'You need it more than I do.'

The next morning, while nibbling his toast, another problem occurred to Finn. If he got hungry sometimes, then so must his tree.

Could he share his breakfast? Did trees eat toast?

Finn took what was left on his plate and ran outside.

He brushed away some leaves at the base of the tree and left the toast on the ground.

He waited a long time, but nothing happened.

'You don't eat toast, do you?' asked Finn.
'That's OK. I'll bring you something else.'

The sun was finally out, so Finn was allowed to play outside.

He didn't want his tree to be lonely so he sat beside it, asking it questions it didn't answer.

He offered sandwiches, which the tree silently but politely refused.

They spent the afternoon in comfortable silence, joined occasionally by a magpie or a small lizard.

That night in bed, Finn couldn't sleep because his feet were fidgeting and his legs were aching. His mother rubbed them and told him a story until he felt better.

'It's normal to have growing pains,' she said. 'It just means you're getting bigger and taller.' She kissed him on the cheek and turned on his nightlight.

Finn lay wondering if trees got growing pains.

If he was growing and it made him hurt, then when trees grew taller, were they hurting too? He tried to imagine his body was a tree trunk and soon felt his bark tingling and his leaves twitching.

Finn decided he would rub the tree's bark tomorrow and tell it a story until it felt better.

Darkness.

All of a sudden, Finn's nightlight had gone out.

His panicky feeling started, but before Finn could call out, something stopped him.

The tree was outside in the dark.
Every night! Was it scared?

Finn slipped out of bed and went to the window. His tree was standing tall and unafraid in the pale glow of the moon. It didn't look frightened at all.

If Tree could be brave, thought Finn, then maybe he could too.

He began noticing the faint moonlight shining through his window; his panicky feeling was gone.

He snuggled back under his blankets and yawned deeply.

In the morning he would tell his mother he didn't need a nightlight anymore ...